Little Pearl's Reflection
"The Light in the Window"

"The Light in the Window," is dedicated to Meg Morman,
my daughter, who is the inspiration for Little Pearl; to Matt Morman,
my son, who reminded me on my 60th birthday,
"You're not done yet, Mom..."
and to Bill Morman (Grandpa), who taught me
that children need love, strong roots, and a firm foundation
on which to grow.

Poof!

CRACK! The loud sound awakened Little Pearl, she opened her eyes to a bright flash of lightning, and then another CRACK! But as she sat up and squinted into the bright sunshine, she saw only blue sky filled with fluffy, white clouds. How odd, thought Little Pearl – there was thunder and lightning, but no storm!

Then as she looked around the meadow, Little Pearl suddenly realized that her Mother was GONE – and she was alone on her 7th birthday!

Little Pearl

Hello! My name is Little Pearl, and that's me in the picture above. My real name is Margaret Sophia Anna Maria Smith, but my parents called me, Little Pearl. On my 7th birthday I had an amazing adventure. I'm much older now, and I'd like to tell you all about it!

My parents are Jack and Anna Smith, and they once lived on a small island in the middle of a big ocean.

Jack (my Father) was a hard-working man, who built stone houses for the people on the island. He used the brown stone from the island mountains, so everyone had a beautiful and sturdy stone home. Anna (my Mother) was a star watcher, who looked at the night sky and knew all about the changing weather. She told our neighbors when to plant their crops, when the rain was coming, and if the sun would shine or be hidden by the clouds.

Jack and Anna also built small purple pyramids out of pieces of stone they found at the foot of the Big Purple Mountain, in the middle of the island. They put together the stone pieces with wet clay from the riverbed of the Old Winding River, that flowed by their home.

After the clay dried in the hot sun, Anna painted star pictures on the little purple pyramids. Jack and Anna gave their purple stone pyramids to friends and neighbors. The Smiths were happy living and working on their small island in the middle of the big ocean.

(Pyramids are large buildings made long ago by ancient people. Often they have a square bottom and four walls shaped like triangles. They have a point on the top, and they are very strong!)

One sunny day Jack and Anna's first baby was born, a little girl (me, of course) with curly, golden hair and deep, sea-blue eyes. Jack and Anna named their baby girl, Margaret Sophia Anna Maria Smith, and lovingly called her 'Little Pearl.'

Little Pearl was their pride and joy, but she was a bit different from some of the other little girls born on the small island. Many had shining dark hair and sparkling brown eyes. Little Pearl had her father's light, curly hair and her mother's clear blue eyes.

As Little Pearl grew, she became strong, adventurous and very curious. At age one, she stood up all by herself, and she slowly began to walk. In a short time she was running and skipping around their stone house. Little Pearl was so curious about everything, especially about the small purple pyramids she saw on shelves near the back window of her home. Jack always put them on shelves to let the clay dry. When they were dry, Anna painted them with star pictures.

At age three, Little Pearl decided to climb the shelves to touch the small pyramids... but just as she reached for the first one, CRASH! The shelf broke! Little Pearl, the shelf, and the stone pyramids all fell crashing onto the stone floor.

Little Pearl wasn't hurt, but she cried loudly as she sat in the middle of the floor and tried to pick up the broken pieces of purple stone.

Anna came running to help Little Pearl, and she lovingly scooped up her daughter - along with some broken pieces of purple stone.

"It's alright, Little Pearl, you see, we can put them together again!" Anna whispered into Little Pearl's ear as she pieced together one broken pyramid, "It's just like a puzzle! You love puzzles, and you can help Daddy and me put the puzzles back together!"

(I was so sad and happy at the same time – I didn't know if I wanted to cry or laugh – so I did both!)

That night Jack, Anna and Little Pearl used pieces of wet, soft clay from the riverbed of the Old Winding River to put the broken stone pyramids back together again. Little Pearl worked very hard, but her pyramid didn't look like the others – there were little cracks all over the place, and she couldn't find the square bottom piece.

(Oh goodness, it was such a mess!)

Suddenly Jack and Anna laughed out loud – smiling and hugging each other. Little Pearl didn't understand. Why were they laughing? Why were they smiling and hugging? It seemed curious to Little Pearl, so she asked in a tearful voice, "Why is Daddy making fun of me, Momma?"

Jack picked up his daughter, hugged her and gently replied, "We're not making fun of you, Little Pearl, we're showing you how happy we are with your beautiful creation! You've given us a wonderful new idea for our small pyramids!"

He took her pyramid that was filled with cracks, without a bottom piece, and placed it over a lighted candle in one of the back windows. Immediately the candlelight began to shine through all the tiny cracks and to make 'light pictures' appear on the floors and walls. Anna clapped with joy, and she too hugged Little Pearl.

Then she explained, "I'll paint star pictures on the pyramid pieces, and your father will cut out the stars patterns so that there will be holes for the candlelight! How wonderful!"

As Little Pearl grew up, she loved to help Jack and Anna build their new stone pyramids and give them to friends and neighbors – they even included a small candle in the gift. Everyone called them: Little Pearl's Light Pyramids. Anna had placed her daughter's first Light Pyramid over a candle in the front window of their house. She knew the light in the window at night would always show the family the way back home.

On clear nights, Anna and Little Pearl walked together into a meadow near their home – they could always see the Light Pyramids glowing in the windows of the neighborhood houses. Anna spread out Little Pearl's old, blue, baby blanket on a special spot, and they lay back close together to watch the stars. The blue baby blanket was covered with colorful star pictures that Anna had sewn onto a gold and white background. Anna told Little Pearl the stories of the stars. Little Pearl learned from Anna how to find the star pictures in the night sky.

(Star pictures are called constellations - I loved all the stories of constellations, and I tried to learn each one by heart.)

Into the four corners of the baby blanket Anna had also sewn star pictures of the four seasons of the year: spring, summer, autumn and winter. In the center of the blanket she had sewn the sun, the moon and Little Pearl's name and birthday.

Margaret Sophia Anna Maria Smith
Twenty-First of June

What fun they had together in the meadow! Anna and Little Pearl watched the stars move across the sky toward the Big Purple Mountain, and then they watched as, one by one, the stars just disappeared.

Little Pearl could hardly wait for the next clear night, when she and her Mother would return to the meadow to watch the stars appear again and slowly travel toward the mountain. She decided that all the stars and the moon slept inside the mountain during the day, and then at night, the stars came out with the moon to help light up the world, while the sun took his turn and rested inside the mountain.

(That's what I thought when I was young. I knew we were the luckiest people in the whole world to see the sun in the day and the moon and stars at night!)

One quiet spring afternoon another wonderful surprise happened - William Charles Jack Matthew Smith was born! Anna, Jack and Little Pearl were so happy to have a baby boy. 'Willy' was an active baby boy, always moving, even when he was asleep. How curious, Little Pearl thought!

(I guess at first I was a bit annoyed with Willy being there and getting all the attention, but when I eventually got used to him, I loved him! I even called him my Little Willy Nilly!)

Willy looked very much like Jack, except that he had bright, green eyes and silky red hair – a bit different from the other babies on the island. Little Pearl found that curious as well. The Smith family was happy in their small island home!

Time passed quickly – as time tends to do - for the happy Smith family, living next to the Old Winding River on the small island in the middle of the big ocean. Little Pearl and Willy grew and grew and grew!

Soon Little Pearl was almost six years old and baby Willy wasn't a baby any more, he was three years old! He begged to help build the Light Pyramids, but he was always running, jumping or playing with the purple pieces instead – pretending they were flying in the air or swimming in the river - so Jack decided to give his son a special job.

Jack walked little Willy along the Old Winding River next to their house, then waded into the water and showed Willy how to dig for handfuls of clay in the riverbed. Willy loved his new job! He would dig and dig, and get dirtier and dirtier, until he had the perfect handfuls of clay, then he ran and jumped home to give his handfuls of clay to Jack.

Jack, Anna and Little Pearl used the clay to piece together the purple triangles that were covered with star pictures, drawn by Anna and cut out by Jack. Little Pearl then placed each finished pyramid on the new shelf by the back window. She carefully lined up the new Light Pyramids so that they could dry in the afternoon sunshine.

Seasons passed: summer rained into autumn, autumn cooled into winter, and then finally, spring arrived. As spring bloomed into summer, Little Pearl and Willy looked forward to the warm, summer days returning. Little Pearl wanted to sit outside in the sunshine and read a new, exciting adventure book that she had borrowed from the island school. Willy was ready to run outside, play in the water, and dig in the clay of the riverbed.

But their sunshine plans were interrupted on the first day of June, as a storm began to form. Clouds filled the sky, and Anna was worried, "It looks to me as if this may be a strong storm with lots of rain, thunder and lightning!" Anna warned her family as she looked at the sky, "It's best to stay inside for a while until it passes."

"NO, NO, NO, not stay inside!" Willy cried out.

"Stay inside?" Little Pearl shook her head. She sighed loudly, "It's too crowded inside for me to read, I can't think!"

Jack was quick to come to his wife's side, "You heard your Mother, both of you, and we're staying inside until the storm passes."

It rained for days and days and more days.

(That's what I remember anyway. I was six years old then, almost seven, my brother Willy had just turned four years old in the spring, and we both wanted so much to be outside.)

Even Jack grew tired of being in the house. His island house building business didn't do well when it was storming. Anna kept her eyes on the sky and hoped for a clear day.

FINALLY the clouds moved away and the sun began to shine! It was June 20th, the day before Little Pearl's 7th birthday and the family's birthday celebration. (I remember it well!)

"Alright everyone, outside we go – but keep your eyes on the sky, and if the clouds return, so do you!" laughed Anna.

Before Anna finished her warning, Willy, Little Pearl and Jack were out the door!

The day passed without any clouds returning to the sky. Everyone enjoyed the warm, sunny day and hours of fun outside. As sunset approached, Anna called her family to come inside for dinner. The Smith family had filled their day with activity – even Jack enjoyed working again – and they were all hungry and tired.

After dinner Anna decided that she was going into the meadow for some star watching.

"Would anyone like to join me?" Anna asked her family.

"No, thanks, Mommy, I'm too tired!" Willy yawned, toddling off to bed.

"No, thanks, honey, it was a rough day at work!" smiled Jack, as he slipped back into his lounge chair.

Little Pearl whispered to her Mother, "I'll go." She missed the quiet times she and her Mother spent together star watching in the meadow.

Little Pearl carried a new adventure book wrapped up in her blue, baby blanket - just in case she might be able to continue reading if Anna was busy looking at the stars. Anna brought along a Light Pyramid and a small glowing candle. They slowly walked to the edge of the meadow as the sun was setting. Anna placed the candle on a flat rock, covered it with the Light Pyramid, and spread out the baby blanket on the grass. Mother and daughter lay back and looked up at the stars – so many were shining that night!

But Little Pearl noticed a cloudy ring around the full moon – a sure sign that rain would return tomorrow.

"It's going to rain on my birthday..." moaned Little Pearl.

"Perhaps," Anna replied, looking at the sky, and brushing back Little Pearl's golden curls out of her eyes, "but we'll see."

Anna moved the Light Pyramid to another rock, closer to Little Pearl, then she got up and walked into the meadow to get a better look at the sky – which was beginning to show a few dark clouds. Little Pearl opened her adventure book and moved even closer to the glowing Light Pyramid.

(I think I fell asleep reading, or maybe I just closed my eyes to rest for a few minutes...but to be honest, this is where my memory gets a little blurry. If you may recall, my story began when the thunder and lightning CRACKED, I opened my eyes, the sun was shining, and my Mother was GONE! I thought she was in another part of the meadow. I was kind of scared. Well, back to my story...)

Anna was nowhere to be seen. Little Pearl jumped to her feet and began running around the meadow loudly calling for her Mother,

"MOTHER! MOTHER! MOMMA! WHERE ARE YOU?"

There was no answer. Little Pearl ran from one side of the meadow to the other side, calling for her Mother. No answer.

"Momma would never go home without me, especially on my birthday! She must be LOST!" Little Pearl cried to herself.

As she stood in the meadow alone, Little Pearl finally stopped crying and decided what she needed to do. SHE was going to go beyond the meadow to look for her Mother!

Little Pearl picked up her adventure book, blew out the candle and blew the wax dry. She placed the book, candle and Light Pyramid in her baby blanket and gently threw it all over her shoulder. Then she began walking – walking toward the Old Winding River that flowed down from the Big Purple Mountain. Her father had always told her that if she were ever lost, she should follow the Old Winding River. As she walked along the riverbank, away from the direction of her home, Little Pearl hoped that SHE wouldn't become lost also.

Soon the sun had climbed high in the sky, and Little Pearl again remembered that it was her 7th birthday! As she continued to follow the river, she smiled and felt very happy. She was on a birthday adventure, just like in her book! She bent over, gazed into the river, and saw her reflection there. She realized that she looked so much like her Mother. In the river water below, Little Pearl saw the reflection of her own blue eyes – which reminded her so much of her Mother that she sat down and began to cry again. How much she missed her Mother, her Father, her home – and yes, even her little brother Willy! Should she turn around and go the other direction? What to do...what to do?

Little Pearl decided to continue walking in the same direction – following the river upstream, calling loudly for her lost Mother. She walked and walked – she called and called. Soon she was growing tired.

That's when Little Pearl became frightened. Would she ever be able to find her Mother? Maybe now she should turn and follow the river the other way...maybe... Just as she was turning around to retrace her steps, Little Pearl spotted a small, white cottage with a thatched roof, surrounded by a beautiful flower garden.

She began walking toward the cottage where she saw an old, stooped woman tending the garden. Little Pearl hoped that maybe the woman had seen her Mother.

As she approached the white cottage and garden, suddenly Little Pearl stopped. She remembered, "Don't speak to strangers", but just then the old woman tending the flower garden turned around and smiled.

Her hair was gray and white, her back was bent, her skin was wrinkled, and her gray-blue eyes were clouded and sad. Little Pearl, nonetheless, boldly stepped forward and spoke clearly, "Hello, hello! My name is Margaret Sophia Anna Maria Smith, but you may call me Little Pearl. I'm looking for my Mother, Anna. If you please, have you seen her?"

"I'm very sorry you have lost your Mother, dear Little Pearl, but as you may have noticed, I am blind and therefore, I have not seen anyone for a long time," the old woman kindly replied.

Embarrassed, Little Pearl turned to leave when the old woman continued, "My name is Cynthia Sophia, but you may call me Miss Sophie."

Little Pearl smiled, "Your name 'Sophia' is just like mine!" Then she lowered her eyes and tried to hold back her tears, "I'm sorry – I didn't realize you were blind. It must be difficult to tend a flower garden that you can't see."

"Yes, yes, my dear, 'Sophia' is a very old and special name – and yes, becoming blind was difficult at first, but now I know each and every plant in my garden by touch and smell," explained Miss Sophie.

"I do enjoy my garden, these are my children now," she continued. "Once long ago I had two children of my own, but today I have my flower garden," Miss Sophie said with a smile as she pointed to her lovely garden of flowers.

Little Pearl felt sorry for Miss Sophie, but she couldn't help staring at the beautiful, yet very unusual flowers.

"Have you ever been able to see your beautiful flowers?" whispered curious Little Pearl to Miss Sophie.

"Oh, yes, dear, when I first discovered my small cottage I was able to see all the colorful flowers. But slowly my sight left me, and I began to know them in other ways." Miss Sophie said quietly and smiled again. "You see, I too was lost when I found this cottage, and I decided to ask the owner for water. But no one was here, so I pumped water from the well for myself. As I drank the water, I became very sleepy and forgot where I was. I decided to go into the cottage and take a short nap, and I planned to leave when I awoke."

Miss Sophie's eyes became sad, "That, my dear, was many years ago."

She sighed and continued, "When I awoke I had no memory of my life, except finding this small cottage and beautiful garden. So I decided to tend the garden each day, waiting for the owner to return. Whenever I worked in the garden and took care of these beautiful flowers, I would pretend that they were all my children needing my care. As I began to lose my eyesight, I also began to slowly remember my past life. When you approached just now, Little Pearl, my memory of my own children became very clear. Thank you for helping me to finally remember!

Little Pearl wanted to hug the sad old woman, but was afraid she might startle her.

"It's alright to hug me, child – how long has your mother been missing?" Miss Sophie asked.

"Since last night in the meadow...when we were star watching. We live a ways down the Old Winding River – my Father, my Mother, my little brother Willy and me," Little Pearl said softly as she gave Miss Sophie a gentle hug, and wondered how the old woman knew about the hug she had just thought of...

"Well, I'm sure your Mother is fine and will be happily waiting for you, once you return from your adventure," whispered the old woman.

"I hope so," was all Little Pearl could answer.

"Let me show you my garden, child – I mean, Little Pearl," the old woman corrected herself. As they walked together around the beautiful flower garden, Miss Sophie lovingly pointed out and touched the lush bushes and groups of unusual flowers as if they were her family. She told Little Pearl their names and explained to her about the care of each one.

The first flower was very unusual because the petals looked like little triangles and were a bright yellow in color. They grew in groups of four as on four-leaf clovers. These flowers reminded Little Pearl of the Light Pyramids her family used to make, except each flower had a green colored star in the center. They smelled like fresh cut grass. How curious, thought Little Pearl.

The second flower group was unusually beautiful because the flowers were little orange squares with bright red and yellow centers. How lovely! The smell of these flowers reminded Little Pearl of her brown stone house with the large hearth fireplace in the middle. Her Father had built their stone fireplace just for her Mother. Little Pearl loved that warm, spicy smell of home!

The third flower grew in clusters of flowers, and seemed strangely unique because some of the flowers were the shape of an " ✖ " and others were the shape of a " ✚ ". They were the same, but different, and brilliant red in color, striped with white. These flowers reminded Little Pearl of the windmills she had seen in her adventure book, and they even smelled like a new book! She loved that smell!

The fourth flower bush was covered in blue - totally blue – shades and shades of blue! The flowers were shaped like little blue moons – all different shapes of moons, bordered in white. There were full moons, half moons, crescent moons, and new moons – how sweet! Little Pearl knew she recognized the sweet smell, but could not place it in her mind. She decided to ask Miss Sophie later.

The fifth flower was Little Pearl's favorite color – PURPLE! Dark purple was in the center and many shades of purple were on the edges. It was the wonderful shape of a heart with large speckles all over, red speckles on some and blue speckles on others.

As Little Peal smelled the delicate purple hearts, she realized that each one had its own scent! One smelled like her Mother, Anna – one like her Father, Jack – and one even smelled like her little brother, Willy, after he ran home from playing in the mud! Little Pearl laughed out loud and wanted to smell more of these lovely purple flowers, but Miss Sophie was moving onto the next flower.

The sixth flower scared Little Pearl at first, because it appeared to be sharp and pointed with thorns. But its color was a bright, beautiful, deep green. As she looked more closely, Little Pearl realized that each bloom also had a tiny, coiled spiral of silky, yellow pods with blue veins running through them. Nothing to be afraid of – the blooms were soft and they smelled like the spring air after a rainstorm – clean and clear and fresh. The lively flowers appeared to be dancing in the wind and throwing their seeds everywhere!

At last Miss Sophie approached the final group of flowers in her garden. They were the most wonderful of all – shaped like stars and each one was outlined in all colors of the rainbow. Some had five points, others had more points, but each had a clear, round, marble-like center. The center marble picked up light from the sun and made the lovely colors appear to be sparkling on the star petals.

Little Pearl clapped with delight as she moved toward the tall bush and bent over to smell the lovely flowers.

Suddenly she stopped, and slowly stood up with a puzzled look on her face. She exclaimed, "Oh dear, they have no scent, no odor or smell at all! I don't think I like these as much as the others."

Miss Sophie just smiled, "You will, my dear, you will. Now please, come into the house and let me offer you a spot of tea with some cookies...didn't you say it was your birthday today?"

(I truly don't remember having mentioned that it was my birthday, but I never turn down tea and cookies, so I happily followed Miss Sophie into the small, white cottage.)

"Come in, come in – welcome!" Miss Sophie sang out sweetly as she moved into the small kitchen. "Please have a seat and make yourself comfortable!"

The small, white cottage was very clean, but there was not much furniture in the room. There was a bed, all white; a table and four chairs, all white; a white sofa and lounge chair and a large white bookcase filled with colorful books of all sizes. On the top shelf were three objects: a white picture frame with a picture of two smiling children, a black jar without a lid, and…

Little Pearl stared at the shelf top. There, in the middle of the top shelf, in front of the only window, was a little, purple stone pyramid, with cut-out star pictures!

(Oh my goodness, was I surprised! How did Miss Sophie have one of our Light Pyramids? Did she know my Father and Mother? Was it a gift? Had Miss Sophie found it in the cottage? I had so many questions, but I didn't want to hurt her feelings by asking! I was also curious as to why she kept so many books and yet she was blind.)

"Do you like my bookcase, Little Pearl?" Miss Sophie asked as she poured tea and served up a large plate of warm, delicious cookies.

"Oh, yes, I love to read! Are those your children in the picture?" Little Pearl asked as she took a bite of cookie and a sip of cinnamon tea.

"Yes, dear, they are, my Matthew and Maria – my, how I miss them now!"

Little Pearl suddenly stopped eating, as she recognized the familiar names that also belonged to her brother and to her. How curious, she thought to herself! "I'm so sorry, and I'm sure they miss you too!" was all Little Pearl could think to say, as she gulped some tea, but then she quickly continued, "What a lovely jar and beautiful stone pyramid!"

"Thank you, Little Pearl, they were gifts that I shall always cherish," replied Miss Sophie quietly. She took a sip of tea, and then happily added, "Now, about your birthday present...how about some flower seeds?"

Little Pearl didn't wish to be rude, but she didn't know how to grow flower seeds or how to take care of flowers at all, and besides that, she was so anxious to continue her search for her Mother.

"Not a worry, dear! Finish up your tea and cookies, and we'll return to the garden. We'll pick your seed presents, and then you may be off to continue your search!" laughed Miss Sophie.

When they had retuned to the beautiful flower garden, Miss Sophie sat down on a white bench. She asked Little Pearl to hand her the blue baby blanket that she was carrying, in order to wrap up some flower seeds. Little Pearl opened her blanket knapsack, took out the book and tried to hide the pyramid and candle behind her as she handed her blanket to Miss Sophie, forgetting that the old woman was blind.

"It's alright dear, I can sense that you received a beautiful gift also," said Miss Sophie as she continued to spread out the blanket on her lap. "Now please, pick a flower of each type you fancy, and bring it to me."

As Little Pearl gently picked the first flower - immediately a new flower of exactly the same type grew in its place - and the flower in her hand immediately shrunk into a large group of seeds, which were the same color and shape as the flower had been.

"Oh my goodness, how wonderful!" Little Pearl whispered as she ran to Miss Sophie and handed her the bright yellow seeds, then thought to herself that it was almost like magic...almost like in her adventure books.

"I didn't realize that was how flowers and seeds grew!" laughed Little Pearl.

(In case you are wondering, dear readers and listeners, I had not done much gardening with my Mother. We sometimes had flowers in our home, but I don't remember my mother ever tending or having a garden.)

As Little Pearl picked each flower, it became seeds and a new, full-grown flower appeared on each empty stem. Little Pearl returned to Miss Sophie with the last group of yellow and white seeds, and smiled.

"Thank you very much, Miss Sophie! I will ask my Mother how to plant these when we get home."

"You are most welcome, Little Pearl. I hope you and your Mother will enjoy them as much as I do!" replied Miss Sophie as she closed up the old baby blanket and handed it back to Little Pearl. **Happy 7th Birthday!"**

Little Pearl once again hugged Miss Sophie, then replaced her book, candle and Light Pyramid into the blanket, alongside of the flower seeds. She closed it up tightly and carefully lifted it over her shoulder, trying to recall if she had mentioned that it was her 7th birthday. She called out goodbye and waved to Miss Sophie – again forgetting that the poor old woman was blind.

Finding the Old Winding River was not difficult because it was still overflowing due to the days of rain. Little Pearl set off again, walking up the river. She was happy that she had stopped at the white cottage, met Miss Sophie and enjoyed the flower garden; but she was again intent on her adventurous task of finding her Mother and returning home.

Just the thought of her lost Mother brought back tears to Little Pearl's eyes...

"Whatcha crying about, child?" squawked a voice from above, "and whatcha got in the bag?"

Looking around the riverbank and into the surrounding tree branches, Little Pearl caught sight of a large red bird flying from branch to branch.

(Here comes another big surprise – have you ever heard of talking red birds...?)

"Well, cat got your tongue, little lady?" called out the red bird again. Little Pearl realized he was talking to her!

"Are you a real talking red bird?" asked Little Pearl, looking up.

"What if I am? But what if I'm not? Does it make a difference?" squawked the red bird as he looked down and winked at Little Pearl.

"Yes, I believe it does," Little Pearl said with a smile, "because I've never met a talking red bird before – or any talking animal, come to think of it!"

"Well, little missy, now you have... I'm Sir J. Ruskin, but you may call me Rusty, now who are YOU?" asked the bird eyeing her up and down.

"Um, well, I'm Margaret Sophia Anna Maria Smith and some 'people' call me Little Pearl. Are you really a talking red bird?"

"Does it make a difference?" Rusty asked again.

"No, I guess not, really, but I'm just always curious," Little Pearl admitted.

"I'd say you are, Pearly! Being curious could be a good thing and could be a bad thing...does that make a difference?" questioned Rusty.

"Oh, my goodness, I'm a bit confused," answered Little Pearl. She paused to think for a minute, then looked back up at Rusty.

"It is very nice to meet you, Rusty – and MY name is Little Pearl," she repeated. "I'm searching for my lost Mother, Anna. Perhaps in your flying you may have spotted her by the meadow?"

"Nope, can't say that I have, Pearly. Did you ask Miss Sophie if she'd SEEN your Mother, Anna?" asked Rusty, laughing so hard that he almost fell off of his branch.

"Well, yes, actually I did, but I don't think it's very kind of you to laugh at blind people!" commented Little Pearl.

"Nah, I'm not laughing cause she's blind, I'm laughing cause she really can see everything – without her eyes, and cause she would've told you about seeing your Mother, without your asking."

"Oh, well, I guess that does makes a difference…" began Little Pearl, scratching her head and wondering what Rusty was talking about.

"Maybe it does, and maybe it doesn't," replied Rusty, spreading his wings and changing branches in order to get a closer look at Little Pearl. "Would you like me to fly along up the river and help you search, Pearly? – I've got nothing else to do today."

"Um, ok, I guess – SEEING as you can SEE more than I can SEE…ha, I made a joke!" Little Pearl laughed out loud.

"Well, Pearly, that's called a 'PUN' not a joke, and try not to do it again, please!" squawked Rusty as he flew into the air, and circled over the treetops along the Old Winding River.

Little Pearl was happy for the company, even if Rusty was a bit grouchy. A long time passed in silence as the two companions made their way along the river. Suddenly Rusty landed on a large boulder and squawked loudly, "Over here, In-Out!"

"What an odd thing to say – even for a talking red bird," Little Pearl said quietly to herself. Then she saw an even odder sight…

(Hang onto your seats, dear readers and listeners - this will amaze you!)

In the distance on the other side of the Old Winding River was a BLUE bunny wearing RED glasses! Little Pearl stopped and could not help but stare...

As she was watching, the blue bunny suddenly began to **DISAPPEAR**!

Then **Poof!** he was gone!

"Oh my goodness," exclaimed Little Pearl, "it must be the bright sunlight, but I thought I saw a BLUE bunny over there – wearing RED glasses!"

Just as she finished that sentence, the blue bunny suddenly popped back in again, next to the big rock where Rusty was perched.

"Pearly, please say hello to **In-Out-Up-Down-Doorknob-Cinnamon-Roll**..." squawked Rusty.

"You may just call me In-Out, my full name is, well, too full, if you ask me. Never understood how I got that name, but it seems so full, if you know what I mean, so "fulllll!" lamented the blue bunny, shaking his blue head so hard that his glasses almost fell off.

"I think it's a wonderFULL name!" laughed Little Pearl, "Ha ha! – I made a pun again, didn't I, Rusty? WONDER - FULL! So pleased to meet you, In-Out, my name is Margaret Sophia Anna Maria Smith – which seems kind of 'full' also – so they call me Little Pearl. And didn't I just see you on the other side of the river before – then you seemed to disappear and reappear over here. You popped 'In and Out', how very curious!"

Rusty was frowning again, but In-Out was smiling and he explained, "Sometimes I get in a hurry and just pop in and out. Nothing to worry about, it's quite alright, you see, I'm a very old rabbit and it helps to get me from place to place, got a few aches and pains, in these old joints, can't fly like Rusty, here, wish I could, but I can't, seems like I can, but I can't – just in and out – pop!"

"Enough, enough, In-Out! Pearly's in a hurry, she lost her Mother, and we're following the river looking for her. Are you 'up' for a little adventure?" asked Rusty as he spread his red wings and again flew high up above the treetops.

"Lost your Mother, how sad, Mothers are very important, of course, should try not to lose them, I'll help! I always help, whenever I can – it's good to help, don't you think? But should we take the Ponte V and look around the Big Purple Mountain? That's usually where everybody who's lost goes," In-Out replied.

"The Ponte V?" questioned Little Pearl. "I'm afraid I don't know that…"

"Pearly, pay attention – it's a vine bridge over there. Good idea, In-Out, let's go!" loudly squawked Rusty as he suddenly descended, and glided toward a beautiful green bridge that crossed the river.

In-Out stepped aside, "After you, Little Pearl, I'm a bit slow at times, don't want to hold you up, I'll just pop along whenever I can."

Then he was gone…

29

Little Pearl skipped quickly toward the beautiful green bridge. It was made of hundreds of vines of different types, winding together to form a footbridge to cross the river. Rusty flew above Little Pearl, and In-Out popped back into sight on the opposite side of the Ponte V.

Carefully Little Pearl walked across the lovely green vines, hoping that she was not hurting any of the leaves as she stepped. Finally as she reached the other side, she heard a whisper, "Thank you! Come back anytime!"

(Ready for another surprise? The unusual is becoming the usual on this birthday adventure!)

"Sorry, did you say something, In-Out?" asked Little Pearl, when the blue bunny suddenly popped in at the end of the Ponte V.

"Oh, no, Little Pearl – that was the Ponte V – you stepped so gently that they were grateful," replied In-Out as he sat down on the grass to rest.

"Oh my goodness, the vines on the bridge talk also," whispered Little Pearl, "how wonderful - I really like it here –
        wherever HERE is!"

"You're welcome – and THANK YOU TOO!" Little Pearl softly called back to the Ponte V.

"Well, don't get too comfortable, In-Out, we have a job to do – let's get on with the hunt! Pearly, why don't you try calling again for your Mother?" Rusty suggested to Little Pearl as he returned to flying.

Little Pearl agreed, and she called again for her Mother, but there was no reply. Again and again she called – but there was no reply. Little Pearl finally sat down on the grass and started to cry.

Rusty landed on a tree branch and scratched his head. In-Out quickly popped over close to Little Pearl's side.

"There, there, no need to cry or worry, Little Pearl, we'll find her, I know we will! Everything will be fine, I know it will. We just have to keep looking. Always keep looking, never, never give up! Look, look, look! Here, now, dry your eyes and let's keep looking," said In-Out kindly, handing Little Pearl her blanket knapsack to wipe her eyes.

"What's in the bag, Pearly?" inquired Rusty again.

"I guess it's alright to show you," sniffed Little Pearl. She dried her tears and carefully untied the blue blanket. Then she spread it out on the ground and revealed her treasures.

"My Mother made this baby blanket for me when I was born – see the beautiful star pictures? This is a little Light Pyramid and candle that my Father, Mother and I made. This is my adventure book, and THESE (she said, holding up the colorful seeds) are flower seeds, a birthday gift from Miss Sophie."

"BIRTHDAY!!! I love birthdays! ♪♪Happy Birthday to You, ♪♪Happy Birthday to You, ♪♪Happy Birthday, Dear Little Pearl, ♪♪Happy Birthday to You!" In-Out sang out loudly.

"Oh my goodness, thank you so much, In-Out – it IS a happy birthday by my meeting both of you, but I really do need to find my Mother today!" Little Pearl reminded them again.

"OK – then pack up, and let's go!" Rusty insisted as he flew off.

Little Pearl began to place her treasures back onto the blue blanket when she suddenly had a good idea.

"I think I'll try to plant a few flower seeds here by the Ponte V and see if they'll grow like the beautiful vines. Do either of you know how to do that?" asked Little Pearl.

"Um, well," In-Out answered, "actually, no, never have done that, sorry, no, no, but it can't be too difficult, there are plants all over the place, right? Someone must have planted them! Yes, yes! Or, no, maybe we can just leave some here and they will plant themselves…" stammered In-Out.

"No, no – give some to me, I'll drop them from the sky and they'll plant!" yelled back Rusty, diving down from the sky.

"Those are two very good ideas, but I really don't think either one of those ideas will work. I think Miss Sophie said that we need some water or something...maybe if I put them close to the Old Winding River near the Ponte V – hey, wait – I'll ask the Ponte V how to plant!" shouted Little Pearl as she ran back to the green bridge.

"Excuse me, Ponte V, my name is Margaret Sophia Anna Maria Smith, and I have flower seeds to plant, and I was wondering if you knew how to do that – plant, I mean."

"We do... Little Pearl," whispered the Ponte V. "Just make a small hole in the earth, place a seed inside, cover it with the earth, add water, repeat, and wait."

"Wait for what?" asked Little Pearl, wondering how the Ponte V knew her name was also Little Pearl.

"Wait for the sun to call them up..." whispered the vines.

"Oh my goodness, so easy, I guess I should have thought of that myself. Thank you, Ponte V."

"You are welcome, come back anytime, Little Pearl!"

Little Pearl smiled, knelt down, and gently poked her finger into the damp earth next to the Ponte V bridge over the Old Winding River.

But which type flower seeds should she plant? She looked at all the seeds. Suddenly she poked a deeper hole, placed a large purple heart flower seed into the earth, and then covered it over with loose dirt. She did this again and again until all the purple seeds were planted. Little Pearl remembered that she needed some water for the planted seeds. Maybe she could use the river water, but she didn't have a container.

"Pardon me again, Ponte V, but what about the water – how do I get the water?"

"Not to worry..." whispered the lovely vines, "it has been raining for a long time, and it will rain another day soon, there is enough water in the earth for your seeds and many more."

"Thank you again! And that's a wonderful idea!" said Little Pearl as she curtsied to the Ponte V. She was glad she had decided to plant all the purple heart seeds next to the lovely Ponte V.

"You are welcome, come back anytime, Little Pearl."

"Well Pearly, are you NOW about ready to continue our searching adventure?" squawked Rusty as he circled around her.

"Please don't rush our Little Pearl, we need time to plant, it's important to do it well, we need to take our time and make sure we do it right, can not ever be rushed, no, no, no, never, never, ever rush planting," cautioned In-Out.

"Oh my goodness, the Ponte V knew my name!" remarked Little Pearl. "And yes, you're right, Rusty! We must continue. I want to find my Mother before it gets dark! Thank you, In-Out, I will never, ever rush planting!" Little Pearl promised as she picked up her blanket bag.

"Then we're off!" yelled Rusty, taking to the sky again. In-Out tried to quickly hop along, but soon shook his head, and just popped out again.

Little Pearl whispered goodbye to the Ponte V and to her purple heart seeds asleep in the earth, waiting for the sun to call them up. She continued walking, calling for her Mother – but still there was no reply.

Eventually Little Pearl realized that her throat was getting dry from all her calling. She decided to stop and have a drink from the Old Winding River. She knelt down, made a cup with her hands, and brought some clear, cool water to her mouth. It tasted very good, and she drank quite a few more handfuls.

(Get ready everyone – here's another surprise – another one you will really like!)

"Sweetheart, please don't drink any more water – too much will make you sick and perhaps even make you – well, you know, bring it back up." said a small voice.

"Mother?" whispered Little Pearl, quickly looking around, "Is that you, Momma?" Where are you?"

"Sorry to disappoint you, sweetheart, I'm not your Mother, I'm here in the riverbed. My name is Olivia. You must be the Little Pearl that the Old Winding River has been babbling about."

Little Pearl looked into the water, looking past her own reflection, she saw a pretty yellow and gold fish with big blue eyes staring up at her. Olivia had orange fins on her sides and orange stripes down her back. As Little Pearl watched, Olivia swam round and round, then flipped over and over, as if happy to have a friend to talk to at last.

"Hello, Olivia, yes, I'm Little Pearl. I didn't realize that the Old Winding River babbled – um - talked at all!"

"Sweetheart, everyone talks! It's just the way it is! Isn't it wonderful?" bubbled up Olivia, as her round blue eyes opened wider.

"Yes, I agree with you, Olivia – it is wonderful!" laughed Little Pearl.

Suddenly In-Out popped in on the riverbank next to little Pearl.. He was huffing and puffing, "We're on an adventure to find Little Pearl's Mother, Anna, and it's her birthday, Little Pearl's, that is, and she planted flower seeds near the Ponte V and..." explained In-Out, taking a deep breath, and then continuing, "would you like to join us, Olivia, and search along the Old Winding River?"

"That's an excellent idea, In-Out! Yes, Olivia, please join us!" begged Little Pearl. She was thankful to have friends with her on her search.

"Olivia can only go so far, Pearly," warned Rusty, circling overhead. "Don't think she can climb the Big Purple Mountain."

"No, sorry, I can't leave my river," Olivia explained, "but I can go along until the river bends as it flows down from the mountain. I can meet you again, after you find your Mother, and return from your climb on the other side of the mountain – if you like, that is."

"I'd like that very much," smiled Little Pearl, gazing into the river and wondering about the mountain climb. "Is it a long, steep climb up the mountain?" she asked. "I've never climbed a mountain before. Are you sure my Mother will be up there, on the Big Purple Mountain?"

"Yes, yes! Just remember, that's where everybody who's lost goes," In-Out reminded Little Pearl, "well, almost everybody..."

"Yes, EVERYBODY!" corrected Rusty, "...eventually. No worries, Pearly, we'll find your Mother there!'

"Oh, yes, dear," Olivia said with a smile, "I've heard the Old Winding River babble on and on, telling marvelous stories of how beautiful it is on the top of the Big Purple Mountain. You can see for miles and miles - you can see our whole island, other islands, and the big ocean around us as well! He claims that on the mountain top you can touch the clouds, taste the snow and ride the rainbows!" Olivia closed her eyes and jumped up out of the water, as if flying, and then gracefully splashed down into the river again.

Little Pearl clapped her hands with delight, and repeated Olivia's words, "Touch the clouds, taste the snow, and ride the rainbows! Thank you, Olivia, I'd love to do all of that on my birthday! Let's go, everyone!"

"Snow is very, very cold, and icy…very, very icy…as I remember…yes, slippery as well. We'll have to be careful and stay on our feet!" warned In-Out, shivering and hugging himself.

Just then a strong wind blew across the river. Rusty suddenly dove from the sky, skirting the riverbank. His head was low, and he squawked loudly, "Earth shaking! Grab a branch! Plant your feet! Tremors!"

Startled, In-Out lost his balance and rolled toward the river. His red glasses went flying into the water. Little Pearl quickly waded into the river and retrieved them. Climbing up the bank, she felt her feet shake. She remembered her Father's warnings about the island tremors - not to panic, and to climb on a large, flat rock for safety. Olivia was already buried deep in the riverbed. Little Pearl wiped the red glasses with her sweater, helped In-Out sit up, replaced his glasses, and grabbed his paw.

"How did you know, Rusty?" Little Pearl yelled, as she began to run, dragging In-Out toward the largest, flattest rock she could find. When she reached the rock, she pushed In-Out up, but 'poof!' he was gone.

Rusty flew back, "Wind was shaking up here - all clear now, it's OVER!."

Little Pearl sighed with relief, In-Out popped back in, and Olivia returned to the surface of the water. Rusty impatiently waved a red wing, motioning for all to resume the search. Together again, the four friends continued to follow the Old Winding River by the Big Purple Mountain, searching for Anna, and enjoying a wonderful, happy birthday adventure.

(That's just the start of my birthday adventure – there's so much more excitement on our journey. Please join us in our next book!)

Love always,

Little Pearl

Dear Readers and Listeners,

   After reading or listening to a book, we often think about the story and "reflect" upon the parts that we liked, and the parts that we didn't like:

   1. What was your favorite part of Little Pearl's story and why?

   2. Was there anything in the story you didn't like? How would you change that?

   3. What do you think will happen to Little Pearl in Book 2: "The Secret of the Smiling Rocks" ?

   On the next page is your first puzzle piece. There are 7 puzzle pieces to collect. Each piece has a part of the special message written by Little Pearl, especially for you. When the puzzle is completed, it holds the entire message, a 'Pearl of Wisdom,' that is the theme or main idea behind the story of Little Pearl's birthday adventure. Whenever you think you might know the puzzle's special message, please email your idea to me:

Sarah@littlepearlsreflection.com

   If you are the first reader or listener to email me the correct puzzle message solution, YOUR name will become part of the story in Book 7! You may email ONE message idea for each book you read.

Keep your eyes open for Book 2: "The Secret of the Smiling Rocks"

Here's your first puzzle piece for:
Little Pearl's Reflection - Book 1
"The Light in the Window"

ALWAYS

CPSIA information can be obtained at www.ICGtesting.com
Printed in the USA
LVIW01n2331280217
525751LV00006B/18